YUCK'S REMOTE CONTROL REVENGE

Illustrated by Nigel Baines

www.yuckweb.com

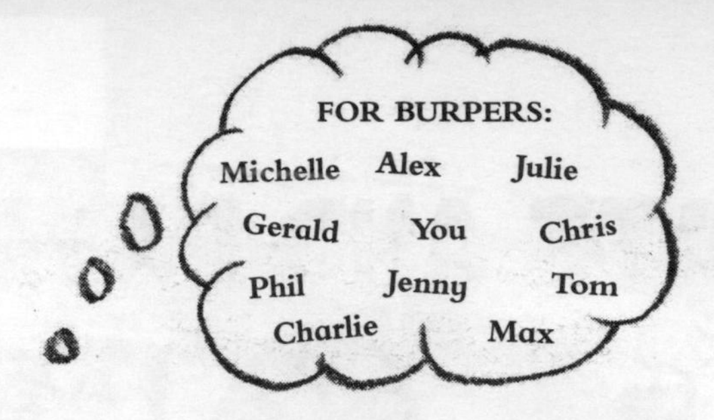

SIMON AND SCHUSTER

First published in Great Britain in 2008
by Simon & Schuster UK Ltd
A CBS COMPANY
Africa House 64-78 Kingsway London WC2B 6AH

3 5 7 9 10 8 6 4 2

A CIP catalogue record for this book is
available from the British Library

ISBN 978-1-8473-8284-9

Printed and bound in Great Britain by
Cox & Wyman Ltd Reading Berkshire

www.simonsays.co.uk
www.yuckweb.com

There was a boy so disgusting
they called him Yuck

YUCK'S ABOMINABLE BURP BLASTER

GLUG! Yuck drank a big mouthful of Coola Cola. He lay on his bed. He could feel the Coola Cola fizzing in his stomach. The bubbles started to rise inside him.

Yuck opened his mouth.

BURP! He did a loud one.

His sister Polly Princess knocked at the door. "What are you doing in there?" she called.

Yuck drank three more glugs of Coola Cola then grabbed his Ready-Steady Stopwatch. There was a gurgling sound in his stomach.

He opened his mouth.

Yuck pressed the START button on the stopwatch to time his burp.

The bubbles erupted.

Three seconds!

"Yuck, are you burping in there?" Polly asked.

"I'm busy. Go away."

Yuck drank ten glugs of Coola Cola. His stomach rumbled. He opened his mouth and pressed the START button on his stopwatch.

Polly opened the door.

BUUUUUUUUUURP!

"Rockits! A ten-second burp!"

"URGH!" Polly screamed, pinching her nose. "That's disgusting! I'm telling Mum!"

She ran downstairs.

Quickly Yuck drank all the Coola Cola in the bottle.

GLUG! GLUG! GLUG! GLUG! GLUG!

He jumped up and down on his bed, and the fizzy drink sloshed around inside him.

The bubbles started to rise.

Mum came running into Yuck's room. "Have you been burping, Yuck?" she asked.

BUUUUUUUUUUUUURP!

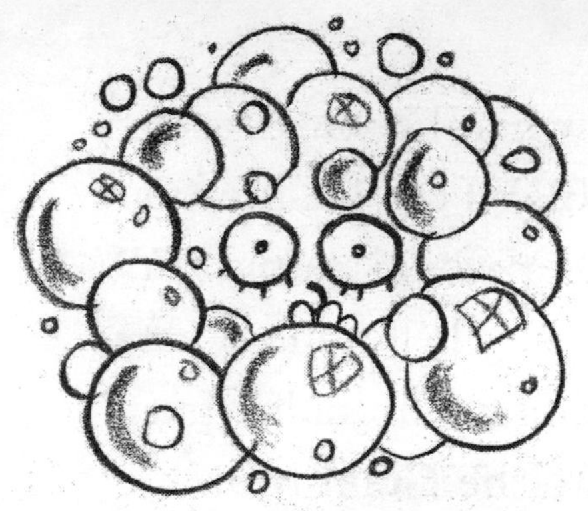

"Phwoar! That's revolting!" Mum told him, covering her nose.

"But I like burping," Yuck said.

Polly opened Yuck's wardrobe door. "Look, Mum!"

Inside was Yuck's secret stash of Coola Cola. There were ten full bottles.

Mum reached in. "No more burping, Yuck," she said, taking all the bottles and carrying them downstairs.

"But everybody burps sometimes," Yuck called.

"I NEVER burp," Polly said. She stuck her tongue out then ran to her room.

Yuck decided that when he was EMPEROR OF EVERYTHING, everyone would have to burp – it would be the LAW. People would burp to say hello and burp to say goodbye, and anyone who didn't burp would be dropped into the Giant Mouth and burped out of town.

That night Yuck lay on his bed clutching the empty bottle of Coola Cola. On the label he read:

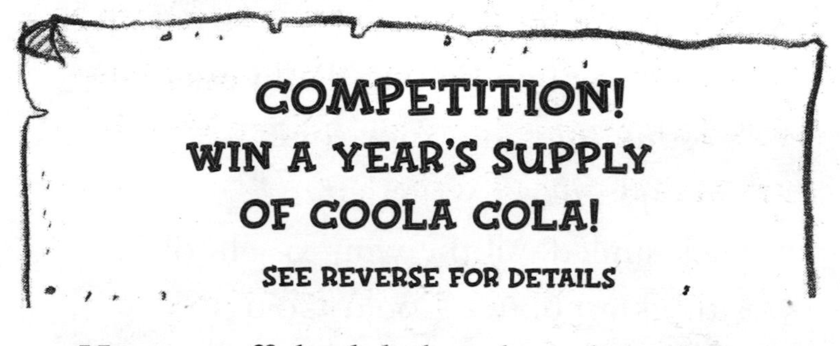

He tore off the label and read on the back:

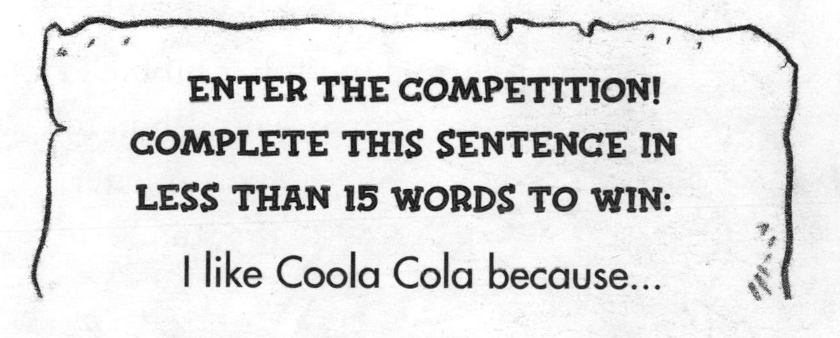

Yuck thought for a second. He fetched a pen and wrote:

it makes me burp

The next morning, on his way to school, Yuck popped his competition entry into the post box.

"What are you doing?" Polly asked.

"Posting a letter," Yuck said.

"But you never write letters."

Yuck smiled. All the way to school he was thinking about Coola Cola.

When he arrived Mrs Wagon the Dragon was writing sums on the board.

"You're late!" the Dragon boomed. She whacked Yuck with her umbrella.

"Sorry, Miss, I had to post a letter," he said.

Yuck sat at the back of the class beside Little Eric.

"Mum's taken my Coola Cola," Yuck whispered.

Little Eric took a bottle from his bag. "You can share mine."

"Rockits!" Yuck said.

Yuck held the Coola Cola under his desk so the Dragon couldn't see. She was writing on the board. Everyone was working in silence, doing their sums.

Using a straw, Yuck secretly sucked up a big mouthful of Coola Cola.

He swallowed.

He could feel the bubbles fizzing in his stomach.

He held the straw to his lips like a pea shooter.

BUUURP!

He fired a burp across the classroom.

"What was that noise?" Schoolie Julie asked.

"It sounded like a burp," Ben Bong said.

The burp hit the Dragon in the face.

"URGH!" she shrieked. She pinched her nose. "That's revolting!"

Yuck and Little Eric giggled.

"Who did a burp?" the Dragon boomed.

Yuck hid the bottle of Coola Cola under his T-shirt.

"Was it you, Yuck?"

The Dragon marched over and whacked Yuck's desk with her umbrella.

"No, Miss. It wasn't me, Miss," Yuck said.

The Dragon stared like she was about to explode.

"The burp must have come in through the window," Yuck told her.

"Through the window?"

"It was the Phantom Burper, Miss," Yuck said.

"Don't be ridiculous!" the Dragon boomed. She poked Yuck with her umbrella. "Now be quiet and finish your sums!"

The Dragon stomped to her desk.

Frank the Tank turned round and whispered to Yuck. "Who's the Phantom Burper?" he asked.

"The Phantom Burper is the most deadly burper in the whole world," Yuck said.

That lunchtime Yuck and Little Eric went to the canteen to fetch some extra burp ingredients: pizza, cabbage, eggs, burgers, fish fingers, onion rings, plum pie, chips and custard.

They loaded the food into their bags then ran to the playground and sat on the bench.

Little Eric scoffed some pizza from his bag then took a swig of Coola Cola.

The pizza and the bubbles fizzed in his stomach.

BUURP!

Little Eric burped in his hand.

He threw it at Yuck.

"Phwoar, a cheesy one!" Yuck said, sniffing.

Yuck gobbled an egg then swigged his Coola Cola.

BUURP! He burped in his hand.

He threw it at Little Eric.

"Phewee, an eggy one!" Little Eric said, sniffing.

Fartin Martin and Tom Bum came running over. "What are you doing?" they asked.

"Burps," Yuck told them.

"Brilliant, can we have a go?"

Fartin Martin and Tom Bum each took a swig of Coola Cola. Fartin Martin gobbled a burger and Tom Bum chomped a fish finger.

They both burped in their hands.

Polly and Lucy were walking out of the canteen. They saw Yuck and his friends giggling.

"What are you lot giggling at?" Polly asked.

"Nothing," Yuck said.

Polly looked at Fartin Martin. "What's in your hand?"

"It's a secret," Fartin Martin said.

Lucy looked at Tom Bum. "And what's in your hand?"

"Show us or we'll tell the Reaper," Polly said.

Fartin Martin and Tom Bum opened their hands.

"Phwoar!" Polly shrieked.

"Uuurrgh!" Lucy shrieked.

"Rockits! A burger burp with a side order of fish!" Yuck giggled.

"I'm telling!" Polly said.

Polly and Lucy ran indoors.

"Watch this," Yuck said. He mashed all the food in his bag: pizza, cabbage, eggs, fish fingers, burgers, onion rings, plum pie, chips and custard.

"It's abominable burp mixture!" Yuck said. He scoffed the lot then he drank all the Coola Cola from the bottle.

The burp mixture and the bubbles fizzed in his stomach.

Polly and Lucy came rushing over with Mr Reaper the headmaster.

"There they are, Sir!"

Yuck held the empty Coola Cola bottle to his mouth.

BUUUUUUUUUURP!

He hid the burp in the bottle.

"Have you been burping, Yuck?" the Reaper asked, marching towards him.

"No, Sir," Yuck said, holding the bottle behind his back. "It was the Phantom Burper, Sir."

"The Phantom Burper? Don't be ridiculous," the Reaper told him.

"The Phantom Burper could strike at any moment, Sir," Little Eric said, giggling.

"If I catch you burping you'll be in BIG TROUBLE," the Reaper told them. He marched back inside.

Polly and Lucy stuck their tongues out at Yuck then ran off to play.

With the Reaper gone, Yuck took the bottle from behind his back and held it up to show the others.

"Wow!" Little Eric said.

Floating inside was a monster burp.

It was glowing and wriggling.

"What's that?" Fartin Martin asked.

"It's horrible," Tom Bum said.

"It's an ABOMINABLE BURP!" Yuck told them.

Yuck pointed the bottle across the playground and squeezed...

BUUUUUUUUUUUUUUURP!

The abominable burp shot out.

"Did you hear that?" Ben Bong asked.

"It sounded like a burp," Bad Bill said.

"It's the Phantom Burper!" Frank the Tank yelled. "It's come to get us!"

Polly and Lucy were playing catch.

The abominable burp flew towards them.

"There's no such thing as the Phantom Burper," Polly said.

The abominable burp exploded in her face.

"URGH!" she screamed. "Who did that?"

Yuck ran off giggling.

That evening, at home, Yuck crept to the kitchen and searched for his Coola Cola stash. Mum always hid things out of reach.

Yuck stood on a chair and opened the top cupboard.

Rockits! His Coola Cola was hidden inside. All ten bottles were squeezed in behind Mum's baking tins.

Yuck reached up, took a bottle down and slipped it into his school bag.

When everyone had gone to bed, Yuck fetched a torch and sneaked outside to the garden shed.

Yuck opened the shed door and shone his torch inside. Coiled in a heap in the corner he saw a dusty old garden hose. He picked it up and took it back to his room.

Yuck had an idea. He set to work on a brilliant invention.

He snipped a length of hose: the burp tube. Then from under his bed, he took an empty bottle of Coola Cola. He pushed the burp tube in its top then strapped the bottle to his back.

His Burp Blaster was ready!

Yuck pulled the sheet from his bed and put it over his head like a ghost.

Tomorrow the Phantom Burper would strike again!

Yuck put the Burp Blaster and the bed sheet into his bag, ready for the morning.

That night, he dreamed he was floating in a big burp bubble. His friends were in burp bubbles too. They floated through outer space to a Coola Cola galaxy. All around, the planets fizzed and bubbled.

The next day, at lunchtime, Yuck, Fartin Martin, Tom Bum and Little Eric fetched more food for their burp mixture. They took it to the bushes on the edge of the playground.

From his bag, Yuck pulled out a bottle of Coola Cola. Then he pulled out his Burp Blaster and strapped it to his back.

"How does it work?" Tom Bum asked.

"Watch this," Yuck said.

He ate a handful of burp mixture then took a swig of Coola Cola.

The Coola Cola and the burp mixture fizzed in his stomach.

Yuck held the tube and burped into the Burp Blaster.

BUUUUUURP!

An abominable burp shot down the tube and into the empty bottle. It floated around inside.

"Brilliant!" Tom Bum said.

Yuck burped again. And again. The bottle was filling with abominable burps.

From his bag, Yuck took out his bed sheet. "We're going to let the Phantom Burper loose."

They all crouched in the bushes.

Holding the Burp Blaster, Yuck pushed the burp tube through the leaves.

Frank the Tank and Ben Bong came walking past.

Yuck squeezed on the Burp Blaster.

BURP! BURP! BURP!

The abominable burps shot out.

"Uuurrrggghhh!" Frank the Tank said.

"Burps!" Ben Bong said.

Yuck put the sheet over his head and jumped out.

"It's the Phantom Burper!" Frank the Tank yelled. "Run!"

Yuck and his friends started giggling.

That lunchtime, they took it in turns to be the Phantom Burper.

Little Eric hid behind a bookshelf in the library.

Kate the Skate and Suzy Shoes were choosing a book.

Little Eric poked the tube through the bookshelf and squeezed the Burp Blaster.

BURP! BURP! BURP!

The abominable burps shot out.

"Uuurrrggghhh!" Kate the Skate said.

"Burps!" Suzy Shoes said.

Little Eric put the sheet over his head and jumped out.

"It's the Phantom Burper!" Kate the Skate cried. "Run!"

Little Eric giggled.

Fartin Martin sneaked to the boys' toilets. Bad Bill was sitting in one of the cubicles.

Fartin Martin poked the tube under the cubicle door. He squeezed the Burp Blaster.

BURP! BURP! BURP!

The abominable burps shot out.

"Uuurrrggghhh!" Bad Bill said. "Burps!"

Fartin Martin put the sheet over his head. Then he peered over the top of the cubicle.

Bad Bill looked up. "Aagghh! It's the Phantom Burper!"

He screamed and did a big poo, then jumped off the toilet and ran out with his trousers around his ankles.

Fartin Martin giggled.

Tom Bum crept to Mr Sweep the caretaker's store cupboard. He hid inside as Spoilt Jessica and the Twinkletrout came walking down the corridor. He poked the tube out through a gap in the door then squeezed the Burp Blaster.

BURP! BURP! BURP!

The abominable burps shot out.

"Uuurrrggghhh!" Spoilt Jessica said.

"Burps!" the Twinkletrout said.

Tom Bum put the sheet over his head and jumped out from the cupboard.

"It's the Phantom Burper!" Spoilt Jessica said. "Run!"

Spoilt Jessica and the Twinkletrout ran down the corridor.

Tom Bum giggled.

All lunchtime, Yuck, Fartin Martin, Tom Bum and Little Eric burped in the canteen, through classroom windows and up and down the corridors. Everyone was running from the Phantom Burper.

Polly and Lucy were sitting quietly in their classroom doing some extra work.

"What's all that noise?" Lucy asked.

Polly opened the door. She could hear screaming from the corridor.

Meanwhile, Yuck was peering in through the window. He poked the burp tube into the room and squeezed the Burp Blaster.

BURP!
BURP!
BURP!

The abominable burps shot out.

"Uuurrrggghhh!" Lucy said. "Burps!"

Yuck put the sheet over his head and jumped up at the window.

"It's the Phantom Burper!" Lucy screamed. "Run!"

"It's NOT the Phantom Burper! It's Yuck!" Polly said. She raced to get the Reaper.

Yuck ran inside and hid the sheet in his bag. The Reaper came marching down the corridor with Polly and Lucy.

"What's going on?" he called. The Reaper grabbed Yuck by the ear. "Yuck, have you been burping?"

"No, Sir. It was the Phantom Burper, Sir," Yuck said.

"It went that way, Sir," Little Eric said, pointing.

"Nonsense!" the Reaper told them. "There's no such thing as a Phantom Burper. If I catch you burping, you'll be in BIG TROUBLE."

That evening, at home, Yuck crept to the kitchen. He stood on a chair and opened the top cupboard where Mum had hidden his Coola Cola. The cupboard was empty!

"Looking for something?" Polly said.

Yuck turned and saw Polly standing in the doorway. She was clutching his Coola Cola stash.

All the bottles were empty.

"I flushed it down the toilet!" she said, sticking her tongue out.

"But that was MY Coola Cola," Yuck said. "I bought it with my pocket money."

"You can say GOODBYE to the Phantom Burper," Polly told him, dropping the empty bottles in the bin.

That night Yuck hardly slept. All he could think about was Coola Cola.

In the morning, he woke to the sound of a lorry pulling up outside the house.

He ran downstairs and looked out of the window. It was a Coola Cola lorry!

A delivery man was unloading a huge parcel.

Yuck opened the front door.

It was a tall bottle-shaped parcel covered in gold wrapping. It was as big as the delivery man!

"Does Yuck live here?" the delivery man asked.

"That's me," Yuck told him.

"Congratulations from Coola Cola," the delivery man said. "You won the competition."

"Rockits!" Yuck said.

A label was hanging from the parcel.

HAPPY BURPING! he read.

COOLA COLA
HAPPY BURPING!

Yuck tore off the gold wrapping paper. Underneath was the biggest bottle of Coola Cola that Yuck had ever seen: a MEGA BOTTLE – a whole year's supply!

"Who was that at the door, Yuck?" Mum called from the kitchen.

"No one," Yuck said. He picked up his school bag.

"Mrs Wagon said I mustn't be late for school," he called.

Yuck reached up and tipped the MEGA BOTTLE onto its side. With both hands he started rolling it down the driveway. He rolled it along the pavement, all the way through the town.

When he reached the school gates he looked left and then right, then rolled it to the bushes at the edge of the playground.

When Little Eric arrived, Yuck showed him the MEGA BOTTLE.

"Think how many burps we could do with that!" Little Eric said.

"We're going to drink it ALL today," Yuck told him.

"All of it?"

"Every last drop," Yuck said. "We're going to make the WORLD'S BIGGEST ABOMINABLE BURP BLASTER."

They hid the bottle in the bushes, covering it with branches, then headed to class.

At lunchtime, Yuck, Fartin Martin, Tom Bum and Little Eric ran to the canteen. They filled their bags with food, stirring it to make a stinky abominable burp mixture.

Yuck crept to Mr Sweep's store cupboard and borrowed all the buckets he could find. He carried them to the bushes at the edge of the playground and lined them up on the ground. He cleared the branches to reveal the huge bottle of Coola Cola.

"A MEGA BOTTLE!" Fartin Martin said.

Yuck, Fartin Martin, Tom Bum and Little Eric all lifted the bottle.

With both hands, Yuck unscrewed the cap and started pouring the Coola Cola into the buckets.

When all the Coola Cola was poured out, they turned the MEGA BOTTLE upside down and pushed in four burp tubes.

"Now let's fill it with burps," Yuck said.

Yuck, Fartin Martin, Tom Bum and Little Eric all sat around the MEGA BOTTLE, holding a burp tube each. They ate handful after handful of burp mixture.

"Ready, steady, go!" Yuck said.

They glugged the Coola Cola from the buckets and started burping into the tubes.

BURP! BUUURP! BURP!
BU-URRRP! BUU-URRP!
BUUUUUURP! BU-UURP!
BUURRURP! BU-UR-RP!

Meanwhile, Polly Princess and Juicy Lucy were looking for Yuck and his friends. They searched the classrooms and the canteen, the corridors and the playground.

"I'm scared," Lucy said. "What if the Phantom Burper jumps out on us?"

"There's no such thing as a Phantom Burper," Polly told her. "It's Yuck."

Behind the bushes, Yuck and his friends were gulping and gargling, chewing and **BUUUUUUUURPING**, filling the MEGA BOTTLE with abominable burps.

BURP! BUUUURP! BUURP! BUUURURP! BU-UURP! BUUUUURP! BUU-U-URP!

They did long burps and short burps, big burps and smelly burps, and burps so abominable that the MEGA BOTTLE started to shake. Thousands of abominable burps were bursting inside it.

"Wow," Little Eric said, watching them. "The world's biggest Abominable Burp Blaster!"

The bottle was so full that its sides were bulging.

"It's going to blow!" Fartin Martin said.

Just then Yuck heard footsteps. He peered through the bushes. "They're coming."

Polly and Lucy were walking across the playground.

Yuck grabbed the sheet from his bag and threw it over the bottle.

"Quick, hide!" he said.

Yuck, Fartin Martin, Tom Bum and Little Eric dived into the bushes.

Polly Princess and Juicy Lucy saw the white sheet hanging like a ghost.

"It's the Phantom Burper!" Lucy cried.

"No, it isn't," Polly told her. She ran over and lifted the sheet.

"Look," she said. "It's a MEGA BOTTLE of Coola Cola."

Lucy stared. "What's in it?" she asked.

Polly pressed her face to the bottle. "Uuurgh!" she said.

Thousands of abominable burps were floating inside it.

Lucy pointed to the four rubber tubes coming out of the bottle. "What are those?"

The tubes led to the bushes.

"Now!" Yuck whispered.

Yuck, Fartin Martin, Tom Bum and Little Eric all tugged on the tubes, pulling them from the bottle.

The bottle started to shake.

“What’s happening?” Lucy asked.

“The burps are escaping,” Polly said, trying to hold the bottle still.

She could feel it rumbling.

“The Abominable Burp Blaster is ready for take off,” Yuck whispered.

Abominable burps were shooting out around Polly’s feet.

Yuck began the countdown. “Five… four… three… two… one…”

BUUUUUUU

BUUUUUUUUUUUUUURP!

The Abominable Burp Blaster blasted into the air like a rocket.

"HELP!" Polly screamed.

She was clinging to the bottle, shooting up higher and higher into the sky.

The sheet was flapping around her.

"AAAAGGGHHH!" she screamed as the Abominable Burp Blaster rocketed over the school.

BUUUUUUUUUUUUUURP!

Yuck and his friends jumped out from the bushes and watched. It was the longest, loudest most abominable burp they had ever heard.

BUUUUUUUUUUUUUU
UUUUUUUUUUUUUURP!

Everyone in the playground looked up.

"What's that?" Ben Bong asked.

"Is it a bird?" Schoolie Julie asked.

"Is it a plane?" Megan the Mouth asked.

"It's the Phantom Burper!" Frank the Tank shouted.

The Reaper came running out of his office. "What on earth's happening?"

The whole school watched as the Phantom Burper rocketed up into the sky, whizzing and burping, spinning and curling higher and higher.

Then they heard a spluttering sound.

BUU-UU-U-U-R-R-R-P-P.

The last of the burps escaped.

Down and down the Phantom Burper fell, spiralling to the ground. It crashed into the bushes.

Everyone ran to see. They heard moans and groans. Arms and legs were moving underneath the sheet.

"There's someone in there!" Yuck said.

"Come out, whoever you are!" the Reaper shouted. He pulled the sheet off.

Everyone gasped.

"Polly!" the Reaper said. "It's you!"

Yuck, Fartin Martin, Tom Bum and Little Eric all giggled.

"Polly's the Phantom Burper!" Yuck said.

"And she's in BIG TROUBLE!" the Reaper said.

YUCK'S REMOTE CONTROL REVENGE

Yuck held a box in his hands. He read the words on the top: X-TREME CHAOS REMOTE CONTROL!

It was the BEST THING he had ever bought!

He had saved his pocket money for three months and now the moment had come...

Yuck opened the box. Inside was a remote control handset, a small electric motor and a make-your-own-vehicle kit.

He read the instructions: Build your own vehicle, attach the motor and watch it go! Racing car! Tractor! Jet plane! You can make anything you want!

Yuck spent all afternoon and all evening glueing together the plastic parts from the make-your-own-vehicle kit.

He was going to make a Yuck Truck. It was like a dumper truck, but yuckier.

He gave it big wheels and a spring-loaded trailer. He painted the trailer bogey green, the doors ketchup red and the cab vomit yellow.

Yuck took the small electric motor from the box. It had four black wires and one red one. He taped the motor to the bottom of the Yuck Truck.

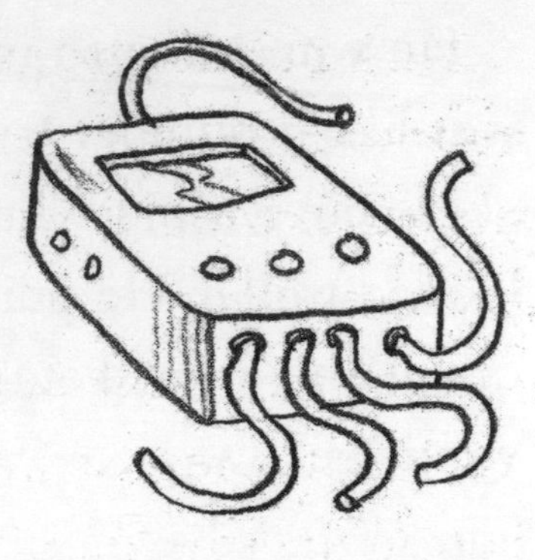

Following the instructions, he attached the black wires to the Yuck Truck's wheels and the red wire to the Yuck Truck's trailer.

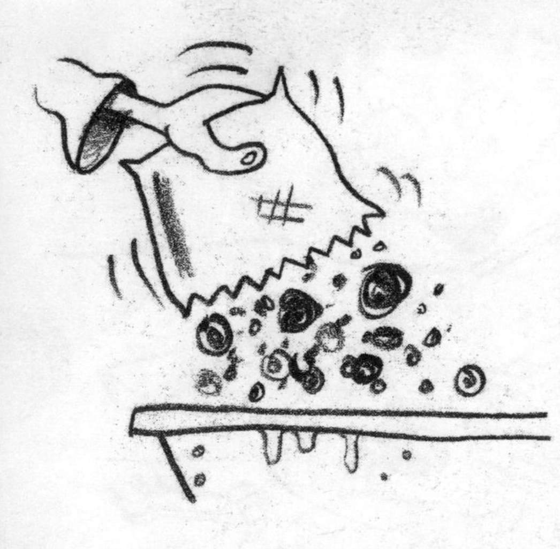

Yuck fetched a bag of scabs from by his bed and tipped them into the trailer.

He picked up the remote control handset and held it with both hands, one thumb over the joystick and the other over the red button – the X-TREME CHAOS action button.

Yuck pushed the joystick forward. The motor revved and the Yuck Truck's wheels started moving. It whizzed across his bedroom floor.

Yuck pulled the joystick back and the Yuck Truck reversed. He pressed the red button and the Yuck Truck's trailer flipped up, shooting scabs into the air.

It was brilliant!

Yuck drove the Yuck Truck around an obstacle course of smelly socks and dirty underpants. He jumped it over a ramp made from *OINK* comics, and through a splash pit of Coola Cola.

He drove it under his bed, across the mould and mushrooms of Swampland. He drove it under his desk, skidding it through a patch of slime. He drove it over the scabs so they stuck to the slime on the wheels.

From the wall by his bed, Yuck picked off a handful of dried bogeys. He loaded them into the trailer. From the carpet, he picked up some chewed toenails and added them on top.

He twiddled the joystick and the Yuck Truck span in a circle doing a wheelie.

Polly Princess walked into his room. "Yuck! Mum says it's bedtime."

She saw the truck on the floor. "You've got to stop playing now."

She grabbed the Yuck Truck.

Yuck pressed the red button on the remote control and the Yuck Truck's trailer flipped up. Bogeys and chewed toenails shot all over Polly.

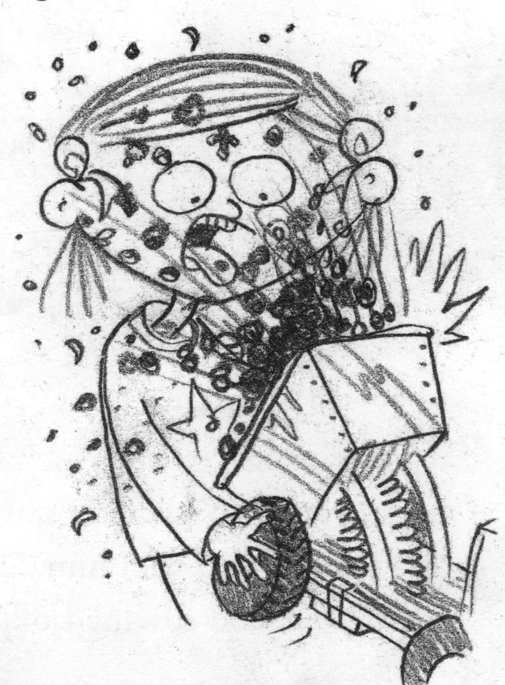

"Yuck!" Polly screamed. Bogeys and toenails were stuck in her hair. "You're disgusting," she said, shaking her head.

Yuck giggled.

Polly threw the Yuck Truck across the room and it smashed against the wall.

"You've broken it!" Yuck said, picking up the pieces. His Yuck Truck was ruined.

"Good," Polly told him. She stuck her tongue out and stormed off to her room.

Yuck decided that when he was EMPEROR OF EVERYTHING he'd live in a remote-controlled palace. He'd have a remote-controlled throne and remote-controlled guards with remote-controlled noses. If Polly tried to attack, they'd sneeze on her, blasting her with remote-controlled bogeys.

The next morning Yuck had an idea.

He fetched the electric motor from his broken Yuck Truck then rummaged in his toy box. He pulled out a toy, his Slime-Ball Snail, a giant snail made of plastic, with little wheels on the bottom and a big shell that unscrewed.

Yuck opened his desk and took out a pot of slime.

He poured the slime into the snail's shell, then screwed it back on.

Yuck taped the electric motor to the Slime-Ball Snail, attaching the black wires to its little wheels and the red wire to the slime-hole at the back.

He picked up the remote control handset and twiddled the joystick. The Slime-Ball Snail crawled across the floor.

Yuck pressed the red button and slime squirted from the slime-hole.

Rockits! It was time to take his revenge.

He drove the Slime-Ball Snail out of his room and across the landing.

He peered round Polly's door.

She was lying on her bedroom floor drawing a picture of a fairy.

Yuck twiddled the joystick and the Slime-Ball Snail slimed across her carpet.

Polly saw it. "Yuck!" she called.

Yuck hid behind the door.

Polly picked up the snail. She saw the electric motor and the wires.

Yuck pressed the red button. Slime squirted from the snail's slime-hole.

"Aaargh!" Polly screamed, as the slime shot in her face.

Yuck came in, giggling.

"I hate you, Yuck!" Polly said.

"It serves you right for breaking my Yuck Truck," he told her.

Polly threw the Slime-Ball Snail at Yuck. It missed him and crashed against the wall.

Yuck picked it up. "You've broken it!" he said.

"Good," Polly told him.

Yuck ran to his room.

He took the electric motor from the broken snail then rummaged in his toy box again. He pulled out another toy, his Bite-me Vampire Bat. It had large wings and long fangs. Yuck taped the motor to it, attaching the black wires to the bat's wings and the red wire to the bat's fangs.

He dashed to the kitchen and fetched a bottle of ketchup. Opening the bat's mouth, Yuck squirted the ketchup inside.

He picked up the remote control handset and twiddled the joystick. The bat's wings started flapping.

Yuck pressed the red button and ketchup squirted from the bat's mouth and dripped from its fangs.

That night Yuck placed the Bite-me Vampire Bat on his windowsill.

It was time to take his revenge.

He picked up the remote control handset and twiddled the joystick. The bat flew out of his bedroom window.

It was dark outside. The bat flapped above the treetops and over the garden.

Polly's window was open.

Yuck sent the bat swooping into her room. He pressed the red button.

He heard a scream.

"Aaargh!" Polly cried.

Mum ran to see what had happened.

"Polly, what on earth's going on?" she asked.

Yuck crept to Polly's door, giggling. The bat was flying around Polly's room.

"There's a vampire bat in my room!" Polly said.

Her neck was red. She clutched her throat. "Help! I'm bleeding! I've been bitten!" she screamed.

Mum rushed over to Polly, ducking to avoid the flying bat, and dabbed her fingers in the blood. "It's ketchup," she said.

The bat tried to fly out of the open window, but Mum grabbed it.

"Yuck!" she called. "Come here at once!"

Yuck walked in holding the remote control handset behind his back.

"Is this your bat?" Mum asked.

"It must have flown in through the window by accident," Yuck said.

Polly snatched the bat and looked at the wires and the motor. "No it didn't. It's your remote control," she said.

Yuck looked at Mum. "It serves her right for breaking my Slime-Ball Snail," he said.

Polly threw the Bite-me Vampire Bat at Yuck. It missed him and crashed against the wall.

Yuck picked it up.

"You've broken it!" he said.

"Good," Polly told him.

"Yuck, go to your room. And leave Polly alone," Mum said.

Yuck ran to his room.

That night Yuck dreamed he was at a remote-controlled zoo where he controlled all the animals. He had a remote-controlled elephant, a remote-controlled giraffe and a remote-controlled lion. When Polly came to visit he pressed the red button and the lion gobbled her up.

The next morning, Yuck took the electric motor from the broken bat then rummaged in his toy box.

He pulled out his Pirate Parrot.

He taped the motor to it, attaching the black wires to the parrot's wings and the red wire to the parrot's bottom. Then he put the parrot and the remote control into his school bag.

On the way to school Yuck searched the pavements and railings, picking off all the bird poo he could find. He collected it in a plastic bag.

When he arrived at class, Mrs Wagon the Dragon poked Yuck with her umbrella.

"You're late!" she said.

"Sorry Miss, I had to pick something up on the way."

Yuck sat at the back next to Little Eric.

"This week we are learning about animals from around the world," the Dragon said, pointing to a big map. "Who can tell me where kangaroos come from?"

Little Eric put his hand up. "From Roomania, Miss?" he giggled.

"Don't be silly," the Dragon told him.

"From Australia, Miss," Schoolie Julie said.

Yuck opened his bag. "Look what I've got," he whispered to Little Eric.

"Brilliant!" Little Eric said, grinning. "An X-TREME CHAOS REMOTE CONTROL!"

Yuck took the Pirate Parrot from his bag.

"What's that for?" Little Eric asked.

Yuck stuffed the parrot with the bird poo he had collected.

"It's my remote-controlled pooping Pirate Parrot," he said.

"Brilliant!"

Yuck held the remote control handset under his desk and twiddled the joystick.

The parrot's wings began flapping. It took off, flying up to the ceiling.

Everyone looked up.

Yuck flew the parrot round and round the classroom.

“Where did that parrot come from?” the Dragon boomed.

“Africa, Miss?” Little Eric asked.

“Don’t be silly! Who let a parrot loose in my classroom?”

"It flew in through the window, Miss," Yuck said.

The Dragon raced around the room shaking her umbrella, trying to shoo the parrot out of the window.

Yuck pressed the red button on the remote control handset.

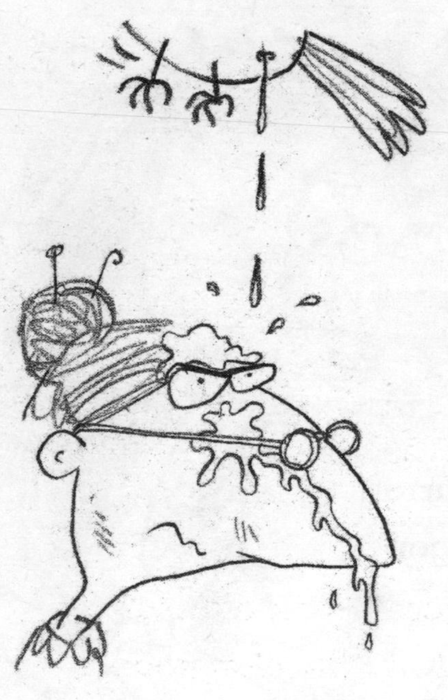

A large dollop of sticky white bird poo dropped from the parrot's bottom.

Plop!

It landed on the Dragon's face.

Bird poo was running down her nose.

The whole class started giggling.

Yuck quickly flew the parrot out of the window and perched it on a tree at the edge of the playground. "We'll fetch it later," he whispered to Little Eric.

At lunchtime Yuck and Little Eric raced outside. They climbed up into the tree at the edge of the playground and sat on a branch, taking it in turns to play with the remote control.

Little Eric twiddled the joystick.

The parrot took off and circled above the playground.

Ben Bong was by the swings eating a packet of crisps.

"Watch this," Little Eric said to Yuck.

The parrot did a loop-the-loop.

Then it did a poop-the-loop-the-loop.

A dollop of bird poo landed in Ben Bong's crisps.

"Uuuurgh," he said, looking up. "It's that parrot!"

Eddy the Egg, Madison Snake and Spoilt Jessica looked up.

Little Eric pressed the red button.

Plop! Plop! Plop!

"Uuuurgh!"

"Uuuurgh!"

"Uuuurgh!"

Mr Reaper the headmaster came running out to see what was happening.

"Now!" Yuck said.

Little Eric pressed the red button again.

Plop!

A big dollop of bird poo landed on the Reaper's bald head.

Little Eric flew the parrot off over the roof of the school.

"Something just plopped on me," the Reaper said, looking up.

"It was a parrot, Sir," Ben Bong said.

"A parrot? What's a parrot doing at school?"

Yuck and Little Eric giggled. They jumped down from the tree and ran round the side of the building.

Yuck looked through the canteen window. Inside, Polly Princess and Juicy Lucy were eating their lunch.

It was time to take his revenge.

Yuck flew the parrot through the window and over the tables. "Bombs away!" he cried.

Plop! Plop!

The parrot dropped two bird poo bombs, one on Polly's tray and one on Lucy's.

Polly took a bite of her burger.

Lucy sipped her drink.

"Uuuurgh! Bird Poo!" they screamed.

"It came from that parrot," Lucy said, pointing.

Polly looked up and saw the parrot flying out of the window.

"That's not a parrot!" she said.

They raced after it.

Yuck and Little Eric hid in the bushes. Yuck was shaking the parrot. "It's empty. We've run out of ammunition." He looked on the ground for some more bird poo.

"Wait there a minute," Little Eric said. He raced to the school gates, then ran back and handed Yuck a curly lump of dog poo.

Yuck filled the parrot.

Polly and Lucy were looking up at the sky. "Where did it go?"

Yuck twiddled the joystick.

"There it is!" Lucy said.

Polly looked up.

Yuck flew the parrot directly above her. He pressed the red button.

Plop! A poo landed on her head.

"Uuuurgh! Bird poo!" Polly screamed.

"That's not bird poo," Lucy said.

It was brown and lumpy.

"YUCK!" Polly screamed. She saw the parrot flying to the bushes. "It's Yuck and his remote control!"

Polly wiped the poo off and ran over to the bushes.

Yuck was holding the parrot, giggling. "It serves you right for breaking my Bite-me Vampire Bat," he told her.

Polly snatched the Pirate Parrot from Yuck. She showed Lucy the electric motor.

"Hey, give that back," Yuck said.

Polly ripped the parrot in half and threw it to the ground.

Yuck picked it up. "You've broken it," he said.

"Good," Polly told him. She stomped off and Lucy followed her.

The next day Yuck ran to class and sat at the back with Little Eric.

The Dragon was handing out crayons. "Today I want you all to draw a picture of your favourite animal," she said.

"What did you bring?" Little Eric whispered to Yuck.

From his bag, Yuck pulled out a black-and-white fluffy toy. "My Stink Skunk," he said.

Yuck shook the skunk and it rattled.

"What's inside it?" Little Eric asked.

"Stink bombs."

"Brilliant," Little Eric said.

Yuck taped the electric motor to the skunk. He attached the black wires to its feet and the red wire to its tail. Then he placed the skunk on the floor.

Holding the remote control secretly under his desk, Yuck twiddled the joystick. The skunk started running under the desks.

Schoolie Julie saw it and jumped. "What's that?" she screamed.

"It's a skunk!" Ben Bong said.

He jumped onto his chair.

"What on earth's the matter?" the Dragon boomed.

"There's a skunk in the room, Miss," Frank the Tank said.

Yuck twiddled the controls and the skunk ran over to the Dragon.

She screamed and jumped onto her chair. "Who brought a skunk in here?"

Yuck pressed the red button and the skunk's tail lifted. A stink bomb dropped out of its bottom. A cloud of stinky gas erupted around the Dragon.

"PHWOAR!"

The Dragon held her hand over her nose. "Evacuate the room!" she said.

Her eyes were watering.

As everyone ran out, Yuck quickly picked up the skunk and put it in his bag.

At lunchtime Yuck and Little Eric went out to the playground.

The Twinkletrout stood with her eyes closed. "Ready, steady, go!" she said.

Yuck and Little Eric watched as Polly and Lucy ran to the bushes to hide.

"Watch this," Yuck said.

It was time to take his revenge.

He placed the Stink Skunk on the ground. Holding the remote control handset, he twiddled the joystick and the skunk ran across the playground into the bushes.

"Coming, ready or not!" the Twinkletrout called, opening her eyes.

Yuck pressed the red button.

"PHWOAR!" Polly and Lucy jumped out from a bush.

"Found you!" the Twinkletrout said.

"That's not fair. There's a skunk in the bushes!" Lucy said.

Polly held her nose. "That's not a real skunk," she said. She picked up the Stink Skunk and showed Lucy the motor taped to the bottom. "It's Yuck's remote control!"

Yuck came running over. "It serves you right for breaking my Pirate Parrot," he told her.

Polly ripped the Stink Skunk in half and threw it to the ground.

Yuck picked it up. "You've broken it," he said.

"Good," Polly told him. She ran off and Lucy followed her.

Little Eric looked at the Stink Skunk. "What are we going to do now?" he asked.

"Follow me," Yuck said.

Yuck and Little Eric went round the corner to the back of the kitchen.

Yuck pointed to the dustbins. "Look!"

Something was moving in one of the bins.

A little nose with whiskers poked up and started twitching.

"What's that?" Little Eric asked.

"A rat!" Yuck said. "Tomorrow we're going to give Polly a surprise."

He whispered something into Little Eric's ear. Little Eric giggled.

The next day Yuck and Little Eric sat at the back of Assembly.

The Reaper was standing on the stage at the front, reading a list of school rules: "You are not allowed to bring parrots to school. You are not allowed to bring skunks to school..."

From his bag, Yuck took out a rubber Rancid Rat. He squeezed it and it squeaked.

"Brilliant!" Little Eric said.

Yuck taped the motor to the rat. He attached the black wires to the Rancid Rat's legs and the red wire to its squeaker. He held the remote control handset and twiddled the joystick.

The rat scurried into Spoilt Jessica's bag.

Yuck pressed the red button.

The rat started squeaking.

"What's that noise?" Madison Snake asked.

Spoilt Jessica opened her bag. "It's a rat!" she screamed.

"How did that rat get in here?" the Reaper called.

Yuck twiddled the joystick and the Rancid Rat scurried off towards the stage. Everyone jumped up as it ran past them.

"Where did it go?" the Reaper called.

Yuck pressed the red button and something squeaked by the Reaper's foot. The rat scurried up his trouser leg.

"Argh! Oo!" the Reaper cried, wriggling and shaking. The rat was squeaking in his pants.

"Watch out, Sir. It bites," Little Eric called.

"Assembly is cancelled!" the Reaper shouted.

The Rancid Rat scurried down the Reaper's leg and out of his trousers. As everyone hurried to their classrooms, Yuck quickly picked it up and put it in his bag.

At lunchtime Yuck and Little Eric took the Rancid Rat to the playground.

Tall Paul and Megan the Mouth were sitting on a bench.

Yuck twiddled the joystick on the handset and the Rancid Rat scurried over to them. Yuck pressed the red button.

"What was that?" Megan the Mouth asked.

Something was squeaking under the bench. They bent down to take a look.

"It's that rat!" they yelled. "HELP!"

Polly Princess and Juicy Lucy were playing Chase the Pony.

Polly looked round. "That's not a real rat. It's remote-controlled! Quick, get it!"

"It's going into the bushes," Lucy said.

Polly chased the rat into the bushes, but it escaped out the other side.

It scurried along the fence and round the corner behind the kitchens.

Yuck and Little Eric followed it.

By the rubbish bins at the back of the kitchens, they saw something scurry towards the rat.

A real rat rubbed noses with the Rancid Rat then disappeared behind a bin.

Yuck and Little Eric hid behind the door to the kitchen. They waited for Polly and Lucy to come round the corner.

"It went this way," Polly was saying.

Yuck twiddled the joystick and the Rancid Rat scurried to the bins.

"There it is! Get it!" Polly shouted.

Polly and Lucy ran to the bins and started looking for the rat.

"Where did it go?" Lucy asked.

Polly saw its nose peeking out from behind a bin.

Polly grabbed the rat. "Got it!" she said.

She held the rat up and showed it to Lucy.

"I hate rats," Lucy said.

"It's not a real rat. It's Yuck's remote-controlled rat!"

Polly looked for the motor. "Where's he put it?" she asked.

"Maybe it's inside," Lucy said.

Polly put her finger up the rat's bottom, searching for the motor.

The rat squeaked.

"Turn it off," Lucy said.

"I'm trying," Polly said.

Just then Yuck and Little Eric stepped out from behind the kitchen door.

"Are you looking for something, Polly?" Yuck asked.

In one hand he was carrying his remote control handset. In the other he was holding his Rancid Rat.

Polly looked at the rat in her hand.

It wriggled.

"That's not remote-controlled," Lucy said.

"URGH!" Polly cried.

The rat raced up her arm, squeaking. It jumped onto her head.

All around her, more rats poked their noses out of the dustbins. They all began squeaking. Then they all jumped.

"AAAGGGHHH!"

AAAGGGHHHH!

The rats scurried over Polly and Lucy, up their legs and across their backs.

The rats' tails flicked and their whiskers tickled.

Polly and Lucy tried to shake them off.

"I hate you, Yuck!" Polly screamed.

Yuck and Little Eric were laughing.

"Revenge!" Yuck said. "Remote control revenge!"